Let's all count our 1, 2, 3's!

1

One whale tail.

Two walrus tusks.

 Three doughnuts.

Four orange stripes.

 Five starfish rays.

6

six rings.

7

Seven jellyfish tendrils.

Eight octopus arms.

9

Nine flowers.

Ten shrimp shoes.

One to ten is fun! Here's five BIG numbers, then we're done!

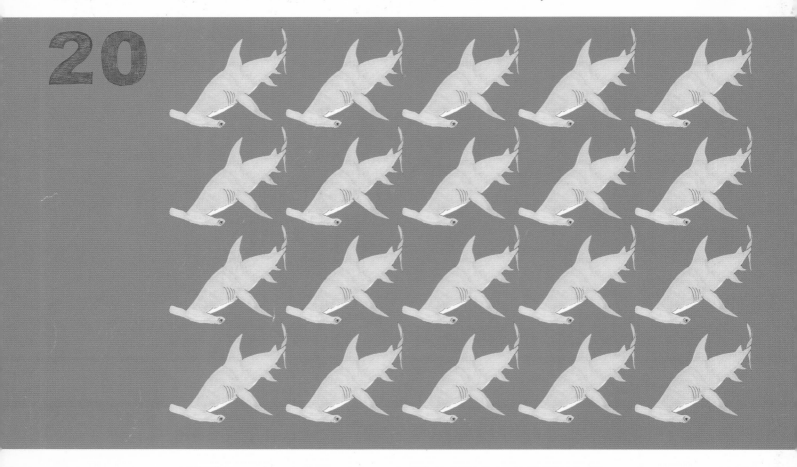

20

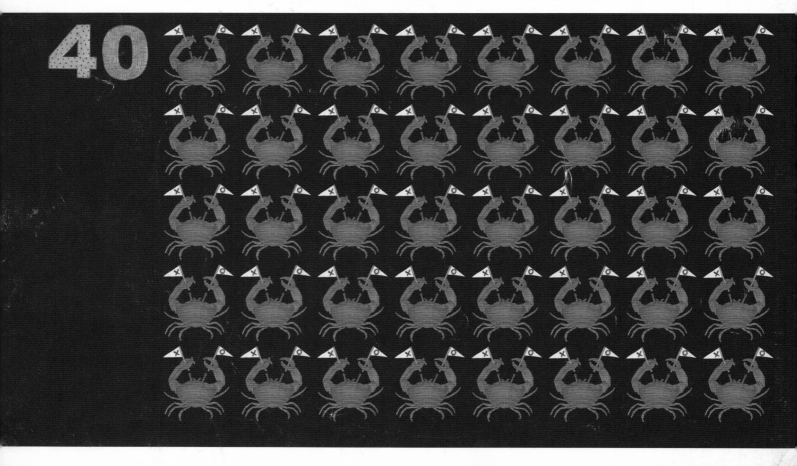

40

60

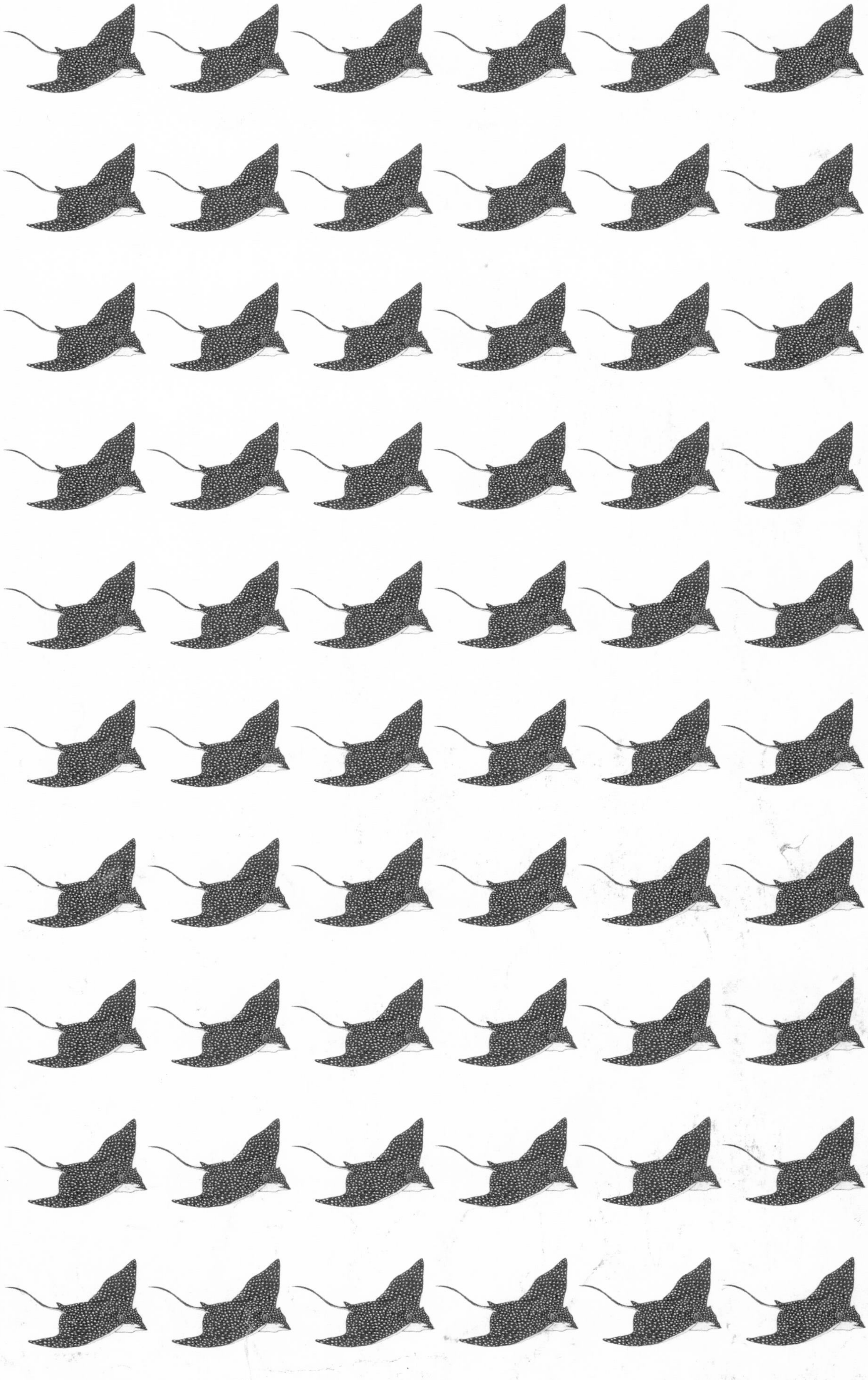

Ninety-nine
seahorses
are swimming
to the right,
and one is
swimming
to the left.
Can you
find it?
Where is
it going?

100

Now find two clownfish that look like this.

Now find four starfish that look like this.

Now find five shrimp that look like this.

Let's count up to 30 different kinds of sea creatures.

1
crab

2
nautilus shell

3
shrimp

4
seahorse

5
starfish

6
jellyfish

7
seal

8
hammerhead

9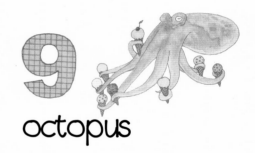
octopus

10
pufferfish

11
sea turtle

12
blue whale

13
walrus

14
sting ray

15
clownfish

16
angelfish

17
orca whale

18
swordfish

19
lobster

20
shark

21
eel

22
penguin

23
clam

24
leopard shark

25
longnose

26
top shell

27
squid

28
dog whelk shell

29
tropical fish

30
dolphin

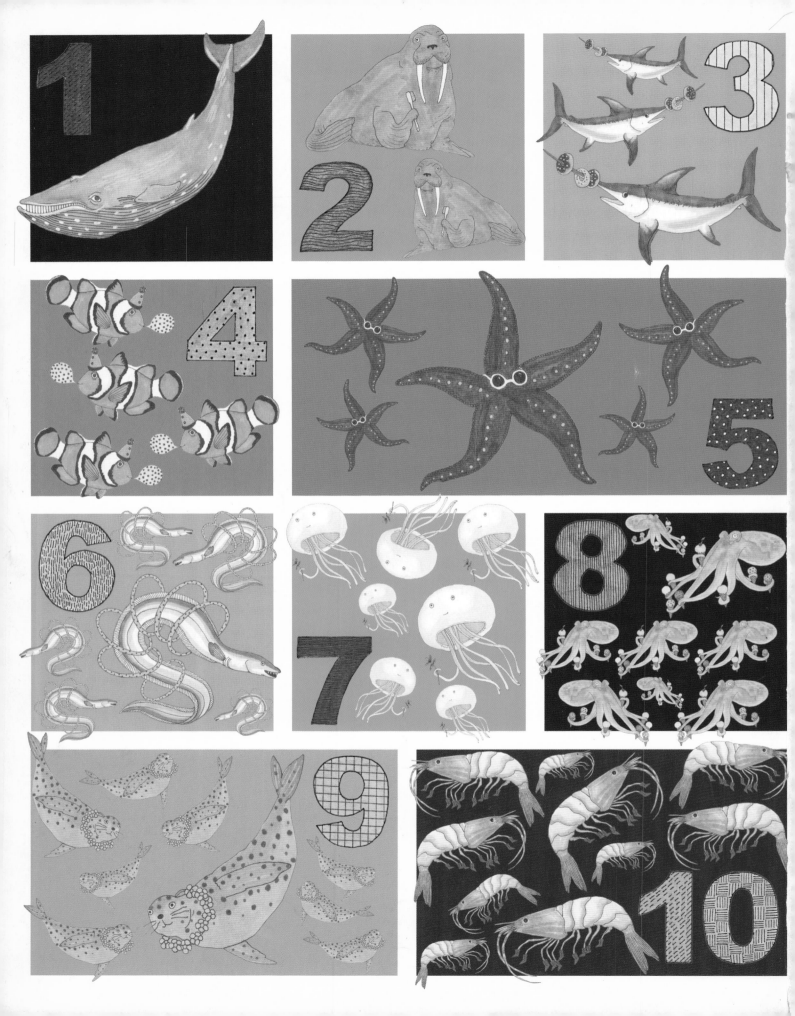